The Glorious Impossible

MADELEINE L'ENGLE

The Glorious Impossible

ILLUSTRATED WITH FRESCOES FROM THE SCROVEGNI CHAPEL BY

GIOTTO

AFTERWORD BY A. RICHARD TURNER, PROFESSOR OF FINE ARTS, NEW YORK UNIVERSITY

SIMON AND SCHUSTER BOOKS FOR YOUNG READERS
PUBLISHED BY SIMON & SCHUSTER INC., NEW YORK

SIMON AND SCHUSTER BOOKS FOR YOUNG READERS
Simon & Schuster Building, Rockefeller Center
1230 Avenue of the Americas, New York, New York 10020

Frontispiece: interior of Scrovegni chapel.
Endpapers: figures from chapel ceiling.

The illustrations in this book were reproduced from transparencies
supplied to us courtesy Scala/Art Resource, New York.

Book design by Sylvia Frezzolini
Title calligraphy by John Stevens
Manufactured in Singapore

10 9 8 7 6 5 4 3 2 1

LIBRARY OF CONGRESS CATALOGING-IN-PUBLICATION DATA
L'Engle, Madeleine.   The glorious impossible / Madeleine L'Engle; paintings by Giotto. Summary:
Describes the life of Jesus Christ and presents twenty-four paintings showing scenes from the life of Christ
by the fourteenth-century Italian artist Giotto. 1. Jesus Christ—Biography—Juvenile literature.
2. Jesus Christ—Art. 3. Giotto, 1266?–1337. 4. Christian biography—Palestine—Juvenile literature.
[1. Jesus Christ—Biography. 2. Jesus Christ—Art. 3. Giotto, 1266?–1337.] I. Giotto, 1266?–1337, ill.
II. Title.   BT302.L63 1990 232.9'01—dc19 [B] 89-6104 CIP AC
ISBN 0–671–68690–9

To
Maria, John,
Bryson, and Alexander

THE ANNUNCIATION

An angel came to Mary. A fourteen-year-old girl was visited by an angel, an archangel. In Scripture, whenever an angel appears to anyone, the angel's first words usually are, "FEAR NOT!"—which gives us an idea of what angels must have looked like.

So the Archangel Gabriel, who visited Mary, greeted her with great courtesy, and then said, "Fear not!"

And then he told her that she was going to have a baby, a remarkable baby who would be called the Son of the Highest.

Mary was already engaged to Joseph. The wedding would be soon. This was strange and startling news indeed. Mary, fourteen years old, looked the angel in the face, asking, with incredible courage, "But how can this be?"

And the angel told her, "The Holy Spirit will come upon you, and the power of the Most High shall overshadow you. And the Holy Thing which shall be born of you shall be called the Son of God."

What an amazing, what an impossible message the angel brought to a young girl! But Mary looked at the angel and said, "Be it unto me according to your word."

And so the life of Jesus began as it would end, with the impossible. When he was a grown man he would say to his disciples, "For human beings it is impossible. For God nothing is impossible."

Possible things are easy to believe. The Glorious Impossibles are what bring joy to our hearts, hope to our lives, songs to our lips.

And what of Joseph, Mary's fiancé? What was he to think of this news?

In those days the punishment for adultery was stoning, stoning to death, and this amazing pregnancy looked to Joseph like adultery. He must have loved Mary very much, because what he decided to do was simply to break the marriage bond quietly and send her away to someplace safe.

But again an angel came into the story, coming to Joseph in a dream. "FEAR NOT! Joseph, son of David! Don't be afraid to take Mary to you as your wife. The child within her has been conceived by the Holy Spirit. She will have a son, and you are to call his name Jesus, 'God Saves,' for he will save his people from their sins."

This Joseph must have been a wonderful man. He believed the angel, accepted the Glorious Impossible, and took Mary to himself.

THE VISITATION

Mary, overwhelmed by all that had happened, hurried off to the hill country to see her cousin Elizabeth. Sometimes it is very important to have an older friend who is not a parent, someone who can be both loving and objective. Elizabeth was old enough to be Mary's mother, but she, too, was pregnant; and when she saw Mary, the unborn baby in her womb leaped for joy. Elizabeth was filled with the Holy Spirit and she, too, accepted this Glorious Impossible without reservation or doubt.

How marvelous! The unborn child in Elizabeth's womb recognized the baby Mary had just begun to carry and leaped for joy! With us it is impossible. With God, nothing is impossible. The stars in the sky above Mary and Elizabeth were brilliant; and the power that created all the galaxies, all the stars in their courses, had come into the womb of a fourteen-year-old girl.

THE NATIVITY

And so he was born, this gloriously impossible baby, in a stable in Bethlehem. Mary and Joseph had to leave home because of the general census ordered by Rome; so Joseph took his young, pregnant wife to register in Bethlehem, because he was of the house of David.

Little Bethlehem was crowded, overcrowded with people coming to register. There was no room in the inn, no place for Joseph to take Mary, whose labor was beginning. How terrifying for Mary to be wracked with pain while Joseph tried helplessly to find someplace for them to stay. Finally they were guided to a cave where animals were lodged. There Mary gave birth to the infant Jesus, surrounded by lowing cattle, by donkeys and oxen. Exhausted, but filled with joy, she laid him in a manger.

Nearby, some shepherds were out in a field with their flocks when suddenly an angel of the Lord appeared before them and the glory of the Lord shone brilliantly all around them. And they were terrified.

"FEAR NOT!" the angel cried, and told them of the birth of the child who would bring joy to all people. They were told that they would find this holy child wrapped in linen cloths and lying in a manger.

Suddenly the angel was surrounded by a host of heavenly angels, singing in a mighty chorus to the glory of God.

When the angels left and the shepherds were able to speak, they hurried to Bethlehem. There they found Mary and Joseph, just as the angel had said, and the baby lying in a manger. They told Mary and Joseph about the angels, and Mary listened and treasured their words. Gently the shepherds placed simple gifts—a lamb, a woolen wrap, a ball—by the baby and then Mary and Joseph were left alone with the child, marveling.

Holding the child in her arms, rocking, singing, Mary wondered what was going to happen to him, this sweet innocent creature who had been conceived by the incredible love of God and who had been born as all human babies are born.

God, come to be one of us.

THE PRESENTATION IN THE TEMPLE

Eight days after the baby was born he was circumcised and he was called Jesus, because that was the name the angel had told Joseph to give him.

Then, at the prescribed time, according to the law of Moses, Joseph and Mary brought the baby to the Temple to present him to the Lord, and to bring the offering of a pair of turtledoves.

There was an old man named Simeon who, like many devout Jews, was waiting for the coming of the Christ, the "Consolation of Israel." The prophets foretold that a savior would come to Israel, and Simeon had been promised by the Holy Spirit that he was not going to die before he had seen the Lord's Christ, the promised Messiah. The Spirit led Simeon to the Temple just as Joseph and Mary brought in the baby, and he recognized the child as the one he had been waiting for all these years.

How marvelous! The old man took the baby in his arms and blessed God and said, "Now, Lord, let your servant depart in peace, for with my own eyes I have seen your Salvation, the salvation you have prepared for *all* people, to be a light to the whole world, and the glory of your people." But he also told Mary that "a sword will pierce your soul," and indeed she was to know much pain during the life of her son.

Joseph and Mary marveled at these things: the angel, the shepherds, and now this extraordinary old man.

In the Temple was also an old woman, Anna. When she had been married only seven years, her husband died, and she lived on to a great old age. She spent much of her time in the Temple, and she came in just as Simeon gave the baby back to his parents; and she, too, rejoiced and gave thanks. How remarkable, how beyond the bounds of ordinary possibility, that two old people should see a small baby and recognize that he was the Light of the World! Was it perhaps because they were so old, so near to the Beyond, that they were able to see what people caught up in the cares of life could not see?

They bade farewell to the baby and to the parents. And Joseph and Mary set off for Galilee, for their own city of Nazareth.

His parents—yes, Joseph was the baby's human father, just as the father of any adopted baby is that child's father. Joseph thought of Jesus as being his very own child, and so, of course, he was. Jesus had a heavenly father and an earthly father, and in Joseph he was very much blessed.

THE ADORATION OF THE MAGI

Very different from the simple shepherds were the wise men who came from three different parts of the globe, a long journey that must have taken them well over a year. They were serious scholars who studied the heavens and the movement of the heavenly bodies. They were both astronomers and astrologers, and we have not seen their like since astronomy and astrology were separated many centuries ago.

The wise men were wise men indeed, men of great intellectual sophistication; but each one saw the birth of an unknown child as an event of unprecedented proportions, and each one left home to make the long trip to Judea because of what he had read in the movement of the planets and the stars. They understood that the birth of a single child could affect the entire universe, just as physicists today understand that all of creation is a single organism. Nothing happens in isolation. The crying of a baby sends sound waves to galaxies thousands of light years away.

So these ancient astronomers believed that something was happening in Bethlehem that would change the world. They met on the way, going first to Jerusalem and speaking to Herod, the king of Judea. "Where is the child who has been born the King of the Jews? We have seen his sign in the East and have come to worship him."

Herod knew nothing of the new king, and he tried to hide his immediate and frantic jealousy of a baby who might grow up to take over his throne. He sent the wise men on to Bethlehem, not far from Jerusalem, saying, "Go and search diligently for the child; and when you have found him, come and tell me, that I may worship him also."

The wise men went to Bethlehem and found Mary and Joseph and the child. Bethlehem was a little town, so they would have had no difficulty asking directions; and all eyes would have been drawn to them in their exotic garments, riding on magnificent horses, with a retinue of servants, and camels and other beasts.

The child himself was too young to be astonished, but Mary and Joseph were awed by this splendid visitation. First the simple shepherds and now these noble wise men— But what could be too great for a child born of Heaven, a child who would always carry a double nature, that of God and that of man.

The wonder of the Incarnation can only be accepted with awe. Jesus was wholly human, and Jesus was wholly divine. This is something that has baffled philosophers and theologians for two thousand years. Like love, it cannot be explained, it can only be rejoiced in. Did the wise men understand this Glorious Impossible? Perhaps they came close. They left gifts of gold, frankincense, and myrrh; and being warned in a dream not to go back to Herod, they returned to their homes by another way.

THE FLIGHT INTO EGYPT

After the wise men had gone, an angel of the Lord appeared to Joseph in a dream. "FEAR NOT!" The angel warned Joseph to take Mary and the child and to escape with them into Egypt, because Herod was going to search for Jesus and slay him.

Again Joseph heeded the angel. He left by night with Mary and the child and headed for Egypt. And so the ancient words of the prophet Hosea were fulfilled: "I called my son out of Egypt."

They stayed in Egypt all the years of Jesus' early childhood. Egypt was a country of pharaohs and great temples and pyramids and the Sphinx.

A childhood in Egypt would have been very different from a childhood in Nazareth. We are not told what happened to Joseph and Mary and Jesus during their years there, but Jesus must have absorbed much, and learned much, because he was a child who was able to look and to listen and to understand.

THE MASSACRE OF THE INNOCENTS

Jesus' birth seemed to Herod a terrible threat to his power—a power that was fragile at best. Judea was part of the Roman Empire, and Herod could remain king only if the Roman rulers permitted. The powerful Roman Empire controlled most of the known world, so Herod never felt very secure on his throne.

When the wise men stopped at his palace to ask directions to the infant king, Herod's jealousy became insane. He called together all his chief priests and scribes, and demanded to know where the Messiah would be born; and they said, "In Bethlehem of Judea, for so it is written by the prophet."

Herod took the wise men and his priests and his scribes very seriously. What was foretold by the prophets would inevitably happen, but Herod resisted the inevitable because he saw this newborn infant as an even greater menace to his power than that posed by the Roman overlords.

In his frantic fear for his throne, he ordered that all babies under two years of age should be killed. Slaughtered.

In our own twentieth century, women and children and babies have been massacred in time of war. Countless children died in the concentration camps when Hitler tried to exterminate the Jews. Thousands of children are being killed today in the wars (many of them in the name of "religion") that ravage our planet.

But the fact that the slaughter goes on does not make what Herod did any less terrible. His soldiers went throughout the land tearing babies out of their mothers' arms. Then were the words of Jeremiah the prophet fulfilled: that there would be a time of terrible lamentation and weeping and great mourning over the death of many innocent children.

Jesus was spared from this slaughter because Joseph had taken Mary and Jesus and fled into Egypt.

When Herod was dead, again an angel of the Lord appeared to Joseph in a dream. "FEAR NOT! Herod is dead. Take the child and return to the land of Israel, for those who wanted to murder him are now dead."

Did Jesus know about all the babies killed because of him?

JESUS AMONG THE DOCTORS

What is eternity?

Who was God's mother?

How many stars are there?

Do numbers ever come to an end?

Why is there war?

How do you know if you're in love?

What is gravity?

Children are full of questions, wonderful questions, unanswerable questions.

Jesus, too.

And where better to ask questions than in the Temple where the learned doctors were to be found, elders who had spent their entire lives in the study of the holy Jewish Law. Jesus was as curious as any bright twelve-year-old child. So when the family made the annual pilgrimage to Jerusalem, he went to the Temple where he astonished the teachers with his questions, and also with his answers. And there, at last, his frantic parents found him.

Was he really gone three days as the Bible tells us? Or was it three hours? It really doesn't matter. What matters is that Jesus was an eager questioner, alert, ready to learn. He didn't notice time passing, or realize that his parents might be worried.

Already he was about his Father's business.

And that business, he was to learn, was not the law expounded in the Temple. That business was not law—but love.

THE BAPTISM OF CHRIST

To be a Christian is to believe in the impossible. Jesus was God. Jesus was human.

This is what Scripture affirms. Yet theologians and philosophers and ordinary people have argued about it for nearly two thousand years. How could Jesus be both human and divine? That he was both is the basic affirmation of the Christian faith.

We human beings seem quite capable of accepting that light is a particle, and light is a wave. So why should it be more difficult for us to comprehend that Jesus was completely God and Jesus was completely human? Of course it takes imagination, but so does it take imagination for us to understand, as we watch a glorious sunset, that it is the planet earth that is turning, not the sun that is setting.

Those are the wonderful things that are beyond ordinariness—like love—that make life worth living.

Even for Jesus, the human being, his understanding of his Godness did not come all at once. There was a glimmer when he was a boy of twelve and talked with the elders in the Temple. But full understanding did not come until he was a young man and was baptized by his cousin John: John, who, years before, had recognized Jesus in the womb when pregnant Mary had visited Elizabeth.

John was reluctant to baptize Jesus, saying that he was not worthy even to lace up his sandals; but Jesus insisted, and as John baptized him in the River Jordan, the Holy Spirit came upon Jesus from above, and a thunder came from Heaven, and out of the thunder Jesus heard a voice saying: "This is my beloved son in whom I am well pleased."

And then Jesus knew who he was: a human being who was God. God who was human. A most Glorious Impossible!

And immediately after Jesus had accepted this Impossible, the Holy Spirit led him into the wilderness to be tempted, for whenever we receive a revelation, it has to be tested. Satan offered Jesus three temptations, and all three came from Satan's hope that he could make Jesus turn away from this Glorious Impossible.

"If you're the Son of God, turn these stones into bread," urged Satan, tempting Jesus with the fact that after his long fast he was hungry and needed to eat, but, even more than that if Jesus would just turn those stones into bread, he could feed all the poor, and everybody would think he was absolutely terrific, like God, not like a man.

But Jesus, who was both human and God, rejected Satan's temptation, saying, "Man shall not live by bread alone, but by every word of God."

Then Satan, quoting Scripture, suggested that Jesus jump from the highest pinnacle of the Temple, saying, "For he shall give his angels charge over you. They shall bear you in their hands lest you dash your foot against a stone," and again Jesus would not be like an ordinary human being.

And again Jesus rejected Satan.

Finally, Satan suggested that Jesus should worship him and then Satan would give him all the kingdoms of the world, and Jesus would not have to die on the cross or endure any of the troubles that come to all human beings.

And Jesus rejected all of Satan's temptations to forego his humanity, and he continued to be human and he continued to be God, and he held to the Glorious Impossible.

THE MARRIAGE IN CANA

There was a wedding at Cana in Galilee, a big wedding, with people coming from near and far. In those days in Judea a wedding feast went on for days, with people eating and drinking and laughing and telling stories. It is quite clear from the Gospels that Jesus enjoyed parties and the company of friends. He also needed solitude, time to be alone with his Father, to "share the silence of eternity interpreted by love." Like most of us, he needed a rhythm of being with people and being alone.

The wedding in Cana came early in Jesus' earthly ministry, those brief years when he called to himself his disciples and his friends, and lived with them, and went about the land teaching and healing. He and his disciples came late to the wedding feast, which had been going on for some time; and the guests had either been making very merry, or there were more guests than had been expected. Jesus' mother met him, saying, "Son, they're running out of wine."

"What does that have to do with me?" he asked, adding, "My time is not yet come."

But his mother, pressing him, concerned for the hosts who were her friends, told the servants, "Do whatever he tells you to do."

There were six large water pots, and Jesus told the servants to fill them with water. In those days water was not pure and was used more for washing and ritual purifying than for drinking. But the servants did as Jesus asked; and when the water was taken from the pots, it was no longer water; it was wine. It was the best wine that had been served at the marriage feast.

It is fitting that Jesus' first miracle should have been at a wedding feast, a celebration of love, and that it was the turning of water into wine, for wine is the symbol of Jesus' blood, of his life that was lived for every single one of us.

Because Christ came to earth to live with us human beings as Jesus of Nazareth, because he was born as we all are born, we are all his brothers and sisters; and that, too, is a miracle.

THE RAISING OF LAZARUS

After that first miracle at Cana, Jesus performed many other miracles. He gave sight to the blind, healed lepers, drove out demons. He raised a young man and a little girl from the dead. He healed the sick, cured the lame. He made many friends, and quite a few enemies who could not understand this strong and joyful man who was a carpenter, who told stories, and who made friends with tax gatherers, and with women, and with all kinds of strange and undesirable people.

When his disciples were asked why he ate with sinners, Jesus heard the question and answered, "People who are well do not need a doctor; people who are ill do. I will have mercy, and not sacrifice, for I am not come to call the righteous to repentance, but sinners."

More and more often he was misunderstood, and the doctors who had marveled at him when he was twelve and had spoken with them in the Temple now began to fear and hate this man they could not tame.

Three of his closest friends lived in Bethany—Mary and Martha and their brother, Lazarus. Jesus went there often, to relax, to eat, to get away from the crowds that surrounded him, clamoring for miracles. And also to get away from his enemies, who were afraid of his joy and his laughter and his constant placing of love ahead of law.

One day Jesus was sent a message by Mary and Martha that Lazarus was ill and needed him. To his disciples' surprise, Jesus did not leave for Bethany at once but waited several days. He knew that he was near the end of his earthly mission and that he was feared and misunderstood by the religious establishment. It was a difficult time for him, a lonely time, because even his disciples, whom he had called to be with him to the end of his earthly journey, did not understand him or what he was about.

When at last he reached Bethany, Lazarus was dead, as Jesus knew he would be. He was dead and had been in the grave for four days. The young man and the little girl Jesus brought back to life had not been dead for long. But Lazarus had been dead four days.

There was a large stone in front of the tomb where Lazarus' body had been laid, and Jesus told the people to take it away. Martha, that blunt woman, put it graphically: "Lord, by this time he stinketh."

Jesus said to her, "Didn't I tell you that if you would believe, you would see the glory of God?"

They took away the stone, and Jesus, lifting up his eyes, said, "Father, thank you for hearing me. I know that you hear me always, but I am saying this now so that the people around me may believe that you have sent me." And he cried out with a loud voice, "Lazarus, come forth!"

And Lazarus, still wound in his grave cloths, came staggering out of the tomb.

And Jesus said, "Unbind him, and let him go."

Jesus, too, would be put in the grave, and a stone would be taken away.

And Jesus would come forth, alive and wonderful.

THE ENTRY INTO JERUSALEM

Jesus knew what his disciples refused to understand or to accept: that when he returned to Jerusalem, he would be returning to his death.

The chief priests and the elders in the Temple were threatened by Jesus' power, by the people who flocked around this strong man who showed them a God of love rather than a punishing god who had to be placated by a rigid adherence to the rules. Jesus' joy was incomprehensible to the priests and the elders, and it frightened them so much that they determined to kill him.

The feast of the Passover was a special day for the Jews, when they celebrated the angel's "passing over" their houses and sparing the lives of their children at the time of their exodus from Egypt. Six days before the Passover, Jesus again came to Bethany to eat with Mary and Martha, and with their brother, Lazarus, whom he had raised from the dead. Mary took a pound of ointment of spikenard, which was extremely expensive, and anointed Jesus' feet, and then wiped his feet with her hair; and the house was filled with the fragrance of the ointment.

Then Judas, who was to betray Jesus, asked why the ointment was not sold for three hundred pence, and the money given to the poor. And Jesus said, "Leave Mary alone. She has done this in preparation for my burial. The poor you will always have with you, but you will not always have me." And his heart was sad, because he knew what lay ahead of him.

Knowing this, Jesus still turned his face toward Jerusalem. And again the words of Zechariah the prophet were fulfilled: "Behold thy king is coming to thee, humbled and mounted on an ass." How strange it must have been for Jesus, who knew well all the words of Isaiah and Jeremiah and Zechariah and Ezekiel, to find their words fulfilled in such a way. He rode into Jerusalem on a donkey (as Mary rode to Bethlehem on a donkey), but he knew he was riding toward his death.

He was an incredibly strong man, Jesus, and he had the humility that comes with great strength.

At first it appeared that his return to Jerusalem was a triumph rather than the beginning of the events that would lead to his death. People cut branches from the trees and strewed them in front of him. Others spread their cloaks on the road. And he was surrounded by cries of "Hosannah to the son of David! Blessed is he who comes in the name of the Lord. Hosannah in the Highest."

How easily and how terribly "Hosannah!" changed to "Crucify him! Crucify him!"

EXPULSION OF THE MERCHANTS

After his triumphal entry into Jerusalem, Jesus went to the Temple of God. His heart was already heavy. He knew that he was at the end of his earthly ministry. He knew that the chief priests wanted his death and that they were powerful enough to see to it that he was killed. The hardness of heart of the leaders of the Temple saddened him. Jesus saw the Temple of God full of money changers and men selling doves, probably for far more than they were worth, overcharging the poor as usual. So he cast out all those who sold and bought in the Temple, and overthrew the tables of the money changers and the seats of those who sold doves, saying: "It is written, 'My house shall be called the house of prayer,' but you have made it a den of thieves."

When Jesus was justly outraged, he had no hesitation in showing it. But after he had cleansed the Temple of the money grubbers, the blind and the lame came to him in the Temple and he healed them.

Everything that Jesus was doing threatened the religious rulers in Jerusalem. He lavished healing love on people they thought were unworthy. He told stories (he was a great storyteller), pointing out that love was more important than law. The angry people in power thought that if they could catch him breaking the law, then they would have reason to condemn him. So they sent some of their disciples to try to trip him up, and they asked him whether or not it was right to pay tribute money to Caesar. Jesus knew they were after him, and he said, "Show me the tribute money." And they brought him a coin. And he asked them, "Whose picture is this on the coin?" They answered, "Caesar's." And he said, "Give to Caesar the things that are Caesar's, and to God the things that are God's."

And when they heard him, all they could do was marvel and go away, leaving him alone.

But the chief priests, and the scribes, and the elders felt more threatened by him than ever, and they met in the palace of Caiaphas, the chief priest; and they plotted how they could take Jesus by subtlety, and kill him.

THE PACT OF JUDAS

Judas is probably the most ambiguous character in all of Scripture. Was he the most terrible villain in all of history, betraying his master, conspiring with the high priests to kill him? Or was he trying to force Jesus' hand, to make him declare himself the Messiah, so that at last the Jews would be free of the Roman yoke?

There were many groups of people conspiring to overthrow the Romans, despite the fact that the Roman Empire was so huge that these people's greatest efforts were puny, like a fly attacking an elephant. But if Jesus should declare himself as the Messiah in a blaze of glory, then the Romans might be forced to let the Jews go free.

There were many people who wanted Jesus' kingdom to be an earthly kingdom, to have him drive the Romans away, and Judas may have been one of these. This is one of the theories about why Judas betrayed his master. He wanted to force Jesus' hand. But did Judas not hear when Jesus proclaimed over and over again that he was here on this earth as servant, not as overlord, that his kingdom was of heaven, not of earth? People often hear only what they want to hear.

We shall never know the real reason why Judas went to the chief priests and said, "What will you give me if I deliver him to you?" They offered to give him thirty pieces of silver, and from that time on Judas sought an opportunity to betray Jesus.

Was it for money? It was Judas who criticized Mary of Bethany for pouring the expensive oil on Jesus' feet, Judas who handled the money for the disciples. Somehow, although thirty pieces of silver was a large amount of money in those days, that does not ring true.

We shall never know.

Like Herod, Caiaphas and the chief priests were afraid that somehow or other Jesus would take away their power, though he had never in any way threatened them—except by his very being. He could look at a person and see whether the heart within was warm or cold, and coldness of heart outraged Jesus. He reminded people, "Judge not, that you be not judged." He said, "As you forgive, so shall you be forgiven." Those were frightening words to the chief priests.

Was Judas frightened, too?

THE WASHING OF THE FEET

It was now the time of the Passover, the time of Jesus' last days.

A party of Greeks came to worship at the feast, and they went to Philip, asking, "Sir, we would see Jesus." Philip told Andrew, and the two of them told Jesus. Jesus said, "The hour is come, when the Son of man shall be glorified. Truly, truly I say to you, unless a grain of wheat falls into the ground and dies, it will stay a seed. But if it dies, it will bring forth much fruit."

What were the Greeks to make of this?

Jesus continued, "Now is my soul troubled, and what shall I say? Father, save me from this hour? But for this cause I came to this hour. Father, glorify your name."

At that a voice came from Heaven, saying, "I have both glorified it and will glorify it again."

The people who heard it said that it thundered. Others said that an angel spoke.

Jesus said, "This voice came not because of me, but for your sakes. For a little longer the light is with you. Believe in the light, that you may be children of light."

Many people believed in him, even many of the elders and doctors; but they did not dare speak their belief out loud, because they were afraid they would lose their positions and be put out of the Sanhedrin, the governing body to which they all belonged.

Many believed. And many did not believe.

And even more did not understand. Not even the disciples who gathered with Jesus to eat the feast of the Passover.

Jesus rose from supper and laid aside his garments, and put a towel about his waist, and poured water into a basin and began to wash his disciples' feet, and to wipe them with the towel.

The washing of feet was an important ritual, and we understand it better if we realize how filthy their feet must have been. People wore sandals, and the roads were full of litter and filth. The sun was hot and the winds strong, and dust would have got between the toes and covered the feet.

So Jesus washed his friends' feet, and Peter said, "Lord, are you washing my feet?"

Jesus gave one of his answers that confused his disciples. "What I am doing, you don't understand now. Later you will understand."

Peter certainly did not understand. "You will never wash my feet!" he said.

Jesus answered, "If I don't wash you, you don't belong to me."

Peter said, "Lord, not just my feet, but also my hands and head."

Jesus said to them, "If someone is clean, all he needs to wash is his feet. You are clean, but not all of you."

Jesus knew that he was going to be betrayed, and who was going to betray him.

He finished washing his disciples' feet. Judas's feet, too.

Then he told them that in washing their feet he had given them an example.

Again Jesus was turning things upside down. He, born to be a king, worshipped by shepherds, given priceless gifts by wise men, was among his friends as a servant. He was like the shepherds who had come at his birth: He would go out into the night, into the cold and the rain, after one lost sheep; and there would be more rejoicing in Heaven when he brought home the one lost sheep than over the ninety and nine who had not strayed. And he was also like the wise men, except that his power came from Heaven and not from earth.

"If you give a little child a cup of water," he told them, "you are giving it to me. And if you refuse to give water to the thirsty child, you are refusing me." And he said, "You have to be like a little child if you want to enter the kingdom of Heaven."

Inside out. Upside down.

Mary of Bethany had knelt by Jesus and washed and dried his feet.

Jesus knelt by his disciples and washed and dried their feet.

THE LAST SUPPER

how strange and fearful it must have been for Judas after he went to the priests and promised them that he would betray Jesus. Did he question himself as to whether or not he was doing the right thing? Was he doing it for Jesus? Was he?

Jesus and the twelve disciples gathered together in an upper room to share the Passover feast. While they were eating, Jesus appalled them all by saying, "Truly, one of you is going to betray me."

Each one looked at the other, sick at heart. Each one knew that he really did not understand Jesus. And they began to ask him, "Lord, surely it isn't I?"

Jesus said, "One who has dipped his hand in the bowl with me will be my betrayer."

They all ate from a common bowl. It might be any one of them. Jesus continued, saying that the Scriptures were going to be fulfilled, as they must be fulfilled. But as for the man who was going to betray him, it would be better for him if he had never been born.

The disciples began to ask each other who could possibly betray their master. They even quarreled—and not for the first time—about who among them was greatest. And again Jesus reminded them that he was with them as a servant, not as a great lord.

And he said, "Truly, truly I have wanted to eat this Passover feast with you before I suffer. For I tell you, I shall not eat the Passover feast again until it is fulfilled in the Kingdom of God."

Then Jesus took a loaf of bread, blessed it, broke it, and gave it to his disciples. "Take and eat this," he said. "It is my body."

Then, after supper, he took a cup of wine, gave thanks to God, and said, "Drink this all of you, for here is my blood, the blood of the new testament, which is shed for many for the forgiveness of sins." Then he told his disciples that they would all renounce their loyalty to him.

Peter said, "Lord, I am prepared to go with you, even to prison and to death."

"And I say to you, Peter," Jesus said, "that the cock will not crow today before you deny all knowledge of me three times."

Judas left the upper room. And it was night.

And Judas went out into the dark.

Into the dark.

THE BETRAYAL OF CHRIST

It was not only Judas who betrayed Christ. It was every single one of his twelve disciples. It was all the people who had followed him from town to town, asking for miracles, but who abandoned him when the chief priests and the doctors turned against him. It was all those who had strewed palms and garments under his feet as he entered Jerusalem. His last few days on earth were days of abandonment and terrible loneliness.

After Jesus had eaten the Passover feast with his disciples, he told them, "A new commandment give I unto you, that you love one another. As I have loved you, so are you to love one another." He told them that he would leave his peace with them. "Let not your heart be troubled," he encouraged them. "Do not be afraid."

Did they not hear? Did they not understand?

Then Jesus went with them to a place called Gethsemane, and asked them to wait there while he went apart to pray. But he took Peter and John and James deeper into the garden with him, and in his desolation he said to them, "My heart is heavy to the point of death. Wait here and stay awake with me."

Then he went a little farther and flung himself on the ground in prayer. "My Father," he said, "if it is possible, let this cup pass from me. Nevertheless, not as I will, but as you will." If Jesus had rejected his humanness, he could have avoided the cross. It was as a fully human being that he begged God to spare him this terrible death. And it was in the fullness of his humanity that he added, "But not my will, my Father. Your will be done."

When he had finished praying, he went back to the three disciples and found them sleeping. "So you had not the strength to stay awake with me for a single hour?"

And he went back deep into the garden and prayed again, and then once more he found them asleep. A third time he went into the garden and prayed, and he prayed with such anguish that the drops of sweat were like blood.

Once more he found his disciples sleeping, and he said, "Sleep on then, and take your rest. But enough. The hour has come. The Son of man is handed over to sinners. Up now and let us go. See, my betrayer is near."

And at once, before he had finished speaking, Judas was there, and with him were men armed with swords and sticks, who had been sent by the chief priests and the doctors of the Law and the elders.

Judas had arranged to give them a signal. "The one you want," he said, "is the one I kiss." So the moment he arrived he went up to Jesus and said, "Master," and kissed him. And they laid hands on Jesus and arrested him.

Jesus' disciples all deserted him and fled. Every single one of them. They ran away from him in his terrible hour of need. Judas betrayed Jesus to the high priest, but the other disciples all betrayed him, too.

His last commandment to them had been to love one another.

But they all ran away from the Source of Love.

CHRIST BEFORE CAIAPHAS

So Jesus was arrested and taken to the high priest's palace. Peter followed at a distance and sat down with people around a fire in the middle of the courtyard, where he could see what was going on. One of the maidservants, who saw him sitting in the firelight, stared at him and said, "Here is another who was with him."

Peter denied it flatly, saying that he did not know Jesus.

A little later somebody else noticed him and said, "You are one of *them.*"

Again Peter denied it, saying, "No, I am not."

After about an hour someone else said, "I'm sure that this man was with him. He talks like a Galilean."

And a third time Peter denied it, saying, "I don't know what you're talking about."

And at once, before he had finished, a cock crowed.

The Lord swung around and looked at Peter.

And Peter, remembering how Jesus had said to him, "Before the cock crows today you will disown me thrice," went out and wept bitterly.

Meanwhile, the high priest and the doctors (who had listened to the twelve-year-old Jesus with awe), questioned him about his teaching.

Jesus said, "I have spoken openly to the world. I taught in the synagogue and in the Temple. I never spoke in secret."

Finally, when no real evidence could be found against Jesus, Caiaphas, the high priest, demanded, "Are you the Christ? Tell us."

And he said, "If I tell you, you won't believe. And if I question you, you won't answer, or let me go. But hereafter the Son of man shall sit at the right hand of the power of God."

Then they demanded, "Are you then the Son of God?"

And he answered, "*You* say that I am."

And they said, "What further need have we for witnesses? We have heard it from your own mouth."

Caiaphas then tore his clothes in the prescribed ceremonial gesture. And they all agreed that Jesus deserved to die.

Peter wept bitterly.

And Judas went out and hanged himself.

THE MOCKING OF CHRIST

The power of the high priest, like that of Herod, was subject to Rome, and Caiaphas did not have the power to condemn Jesus to death; only Rome could pass the death sentence. So Caiaphas sent Jesus to Pontius Pilate, the Roman governor.

Pilate questioned Jesus, "Don't you know that I have the power to condemn you to death?"

Jesus answered, "You would have no power over me at all if it were not given you by Heaven."

Pilate was impressed by Jesus, by his *real*ness, his indifference to worldly power. He was so moved by the extraordinary quality of truth which he felt in Jesus that he wanted to release him. But Jesus' antagonists shouted, "If you free this man, you are not Caesar's friend. Anyone who claims to be a king, as this man does, is defying Caesar."

Pilate was torn. His wife, Claudia, had urged him to set Jesus free. But Pilate dared not be accused of going against Rome.

Still, he tried. During the festival season it was the custom that one prisoner chosen by the people should be released, and Pilate offered to release Jesus. But the people, stirred up by the high priest and the elders, shouted, "Not Jesus! Bar-Abbas!"

So it was Bar-Abbas who was freed. We know little about Bar-Abbas except that he was reputed to have revolted against Rome, and to have murdered. And the name *Bar-Abbas* means "son of the father." There is a wild irony in this, because Jesus always referred to himself as "Son of man," thereby proclaiming himself as brother to all human beings. Did Bar-Abbas think of himself as the Son of the Father? How did he feel when he was let out of prison and Jesus was led to the cross?

Reluctantly, Pilate turned Jesus over to the soldiers, who stripped him of his own clothes and dressed him in scarlet. They put a crown of thorns on his head and a reed in his hand, and jeered at him: "Hail, King of the Jews!" They spat at him, took the reed, and hit him with it. How is it that human beings find it easy and even, alas, pleasurable to hurt another human being? Jesus came to live with us to show us how to be human, truly human; and for this love he was betrayed, mocked, feared.

Will we ever learn to be human?

THE ROAD TO CALVARY

Beaten, betrayed, exhausted, Jesus was forced to carry his own cross. Under its weight he slipped and fell, and a man called Simon, who came from Cyrene, carried the cross part of the way for Jesus.

Jesus, stumbling along, not too proud to allow Simon to help him, was followed by a crowd, some mocking him, some weeping and wailing. As he staggered up the hill, a woman named Veronica compassionately wiped the sweat from his face.

Where were the disciples? Most of them were in hiding, afraid for their lives.

It was a lonely journey. Abandoned, Jesus climbed the weary way to Golgotha, which means "the place of the skull."

There is a story that the skull for which Golgotha was named was Adam's skull, and that Jesus' cross was made from the wood of the tree of the knowledge of good and evil.

The first Adam, the first Son of man, had turned away from God. Jesus, often called the Second Adam, bent under the weight of the cross, held true. He was the Son of man, but wherever he went, he went to his Father.

THE CRUCIFIXION

Over Jesus' cross Pilate had prepared a sign that read JESUS OF NAZARETH, THE KING OF THE JEWS. The chief priests, rejecting any possibility that Jesus was a king, asked Pilate to change it; but Pilate said, "What I have written, I have written."

Jesus was nailed to the cross, and on either side of him a thief was also being crucified. One of the thieves joined with the crowd in taunting him.

"Are you not the Christ? Save yourself and us."

The other thief said, "Have you no fear of God? We deserve our sentences. But *he* did nothing wrong." And he said, "Jesus, remember me when you come into your kingdom."

Jesus said to this thief, "I tell you truly, today you will be with me in Paradise." He looked at the crowd screaming obscenities at him, and said, "Father, forgive them, for they do not know what they are doing."

They did not know. The disciples did not know. Only one of the twelve was with Jesus on that terrible day. John. John was there. And the women. The women were with Jesus while he died, his mother and Mary Magdalen; all the women who had been with him, caring for him while he was alive, were with him now at his end. How exquisite was Mary's pain as the sword of anguish went through her heart as she watched her son dying.

The sky darkened and the earth quaked. The curtain of the Temple was torn in two by an invisible force. And in the darkness Jesus cried out, "My God, my God, why have you forsaken me?"

And then there was darkness, and silence broken only by weeping. Darkness. Silence.

Jesus cried out with a loud voice, "Father, into your hands I commend my spirit!" And then he breathed his last.

That Jesus on the cross should have been able to cry out with a loud voice is a reminder that he was a very strong man, for death by crucifixion collapses the lungs. And this strong man was faithful to the last.

We need not try to reconcile the two aspects of Jesus, human and divine. It cannot be done. We need only know that his was a love that shows us all how to love.

THE LAMENTATION

Jesus was taken down from the cross and put in his mother's arms, and she held the body of the son she had borne.

Jesus still had some friends among the doctors and the elders, men who dared not acknowledge him publicly. One of them, Joseph of Arimathaea, asked Pilate for permission to remove Jesus' body and lay it in his own tomb, and Pilate agreed. Another of the elders, Nicodemus (who had come to speak to Jesus at night because he was afraid of criticism), came with about a hundred pounds of myrrh and aloes, which were used for anointing dead bodies with fragrance. Where was the myrrh that had been brought to Jesus by the wise men when he was a baby?

So Jesus' body was wrapped in strips of linen, anointed with spices, and laid in the tomb—the body of a king whose kingdom was not an earthly one of power and might, but a kingdom whose king was acquainted with grief, and who came to earth to save sinners and sick and broken people with a love freely given—a love so free that it was not understood by those who like to put a price on everything.

The women who had loved Jesus, who had waited with him through his dying, followed Joseph and watched while Jesus' body was put into the tomb. The sun had moved across the sky and set in the west, and it was now the Sabbath day, when Jesus' followers rested from work, according to the commandment.

Mary, her arms forever empty of the son she had borne, was with John, sharing grief.

Judas was dead.

The other ten were hiding and afraid.

It was a terrible time.

THE RESURRECTION

The first of the gloriously impossible things that Jesus did was to be born—the power that created the universe come to live with us as one of us. And now his time on earth was over, and in the eyes of the religious establishment of his day, he had failed and they had triumphed. True, he had healed a few cripples and lepers, given sight to a few blind people, driven out a few demons; but he threatened the religious establishment and they killed him. Or thought they did.

Mary of Magdala, grieving, went to the tomb where Jesus had been laid, and—lo!—he was not there, and she was terrified. She saw a man and approached him, thinking that he was a gardener, and asked after Jesus.

And the man called her by name, "Mary!"

And she knew him and rushed to him in joy, and he stopped her, saying, "Do not touch me yet!"

He had just emerged from death and from the tomb. After his resurrection he was never recognized by sight, but by his voice, or in the breaking of bread, the eating of fish. Mary was the first person to see him and it may well be that if she had touched him at that moment it would have killed her. It was not yet safe to touch him.

But she knew him!

Christ was dead.

Christ was risen!

Alleluia!

THE ASCENSION

It was a long time before all the disciples and Jesus' other friends were able to believe in this wondrously impossible thing that had happened! He appeared to two men on their way to Emmaus who did not recognize him until they stopped to eat and he broke the bread and gave the blessing. He appeared to the disciples when they were standing on a beach, and they were terrified, thinking that he was a ghost. He said, "Why are you so frightened? Look at me!" And he asked them for something to eat, and they gave him a piece of fish they had just cooked; and he took it and ate it before their very eyes. Thomas, his disciple, would not believe that the Lord was risen until he saw Jesus for himself and touched his wounds.

But when they all believed, of course they wanted him to stay with them forever. Well before the terrible day of the crucifixion, Jesus had told his disciples, "Listen, it is best for you if I go away. If I don't leave you, the Comforter will not come to you, but if I leave, I will send the Comforter to you." The Comforter, the Holy Spirit, the third person of the indivisible Trinity. And, as always, the disciples did not understand. Even though they did not recognize the risen body until Christ spoke, or ate, or called them, they wanted to cling, to keep him with them.

But Jesus led them to Bethany, where Mary and Martha and Lazarus lived, and he blessed them, and then he was parted from them and was carried up into Heaven.

How? We don't know. With us such things are impossible. With God nothing is impossible.

Alleluia!

PENTECOST

Pentecost was an ancient festival that had been observed by the Jews for many centuries. Originally it was probably a festival of thanksgiving for the first fruits, the early harvest. Later it came to be an observance of thanksgiving for the great gift of the Torah.

On the day of the Pentecost, after Jesus had ascended into Heaven, the disciples and many of Jesus' friends were gathered together when suddenly there came a sound from Heaven as of a rushing mighty wind, and it filled the house where they were sitting. And there appeared to them cloven tongues like flames, and the flames rested on each one of them.

It was a glorious time!

There were many Jews in Jerusalem at that time, from every nation under Heaven, people who spoke many different languages. And they were astounded, because they all heard the disciples speaking in their own language, and they asked, "Aren't all these people who are speaking to us Galileans? How is it that we each hear our own language? What does all this mean?"

It was the fulfilling of Jesus' promise, that he must leave his friends but that the Holy Spirit, the Comforter, the strength-giver, would come to give them peace and joy.

"Let not your heart be troubled," Jesus had said. "The Comforter will teach you all things. Peace I leave with you, my peace I give to you. I am giving you a new commandment, that you love one another. As I have loved you, so must you love each other. People will know that you are my disciples if you love one another."

Jesus came to us for love, and he died for us for love, and he rose from the grave for love, and he ascended into Heaven for love, and the Comforter came to us to teach us love.

So, beloveds, let us love one another as Jesus has called us to do.

Amen. Alleluia! Amen.

GIOTTO AND THE SCROVEGNI CHAPEL

At his death in 1337, Giotto was famous throughout Italy. He was acclaimed as the artist who had revived painting from its long sleep, whose brush created figures that truly seemed to live and breathe.

The little Scrovegni Chapel in Padua, decorated by the Florentine Giotto nearly seven hundred years ago (around 1304), suggests why Giotto enjoyed, and still enjoys, such a grand reputation. The banker Enrico Scrovegni offered the chapel and its frescoes (wall paintings on plaster) to Mary and Jesus, in the hope that this good work might help pay for the sins of Enrico's father, an infamous moneylender who had violated the Christian faith.

Giotto frescoed the Christian story from its beginning in the life of Mary to its close in the Last Judgment. Some forty scenes tell this holy story, and it is from them that this book's illustrations are chosen.

What was it that Giotto's contemporaries found so wonderful in his art? It surely was the feeling that his Biblical stories, from a time long ago, were believable in ordinary human terms in the here-and-now. Above all, Giotto's art is about people meeting; a joyous hello (*Visitation*), a tragic final goodbye (*Lamentation*), a solemn expression of love (*Adoration of the Magi*), a criminal violation of friendship (*Betrayal of Christ*). In less dramatic terms, aren't your life and mine, stories of hellos and goodbyes?

A painter's task, unlike a writer who is able to describe at length, is to make an emotional situation understandable at a glance. Before Giotto, paintings tended to flat pattern, arrangements of color against a gold ground. Giotto's revolutionary idea was to take the three-dimensional solidity and weightiness of the sculpture of his day, and to translate it into painting. He paints the surface away, and we seem to look through a window at a shallow stage where physically believable people are gathered, people we can almost touch.

Beyond a physical truth, Giotto's scenes have an emotional truth. This is achieved not so much through facial expression—his faces seem very much alike—as by gesture, posture, and the relations of figures one to the other. See, for instance, how the arrangement of the figures in *The Lamentation* along with lines of the barren landscape are calculated to lead our eyes to the intimate embrace of a grieving mother and her dead son.

Powerful human feelings in physically believable bodies—now that was something that had not been seen for many centuries in Giotto's Italy. Small wonder that his contemporaries saw in Giotto an artist, and a man, who had reached for the Glorious Impossible.

A. RICHARD TURNER